Abigail's Chickens

Illustrated by
Mary Rensberry

Richard Rensberry

Published by: QuickTurtle Books LLC®

http://www.richardrensberry.com

ISBN: 978-1-940736-34-1
Published in the United States of America

SALLY CLUCKS,
QUEENIE SINGS,

GERTRUDE SQUAWKS
AND FLAPS HER WINGS.

IT'S SUN UP TIME
ON A SUMMER MORN,
THE HENS GET WATERED
AND FED SWEET CORN.

THE DOVES GO COO
FROM THE FIELDS OF HAY;
ABIGAIL'S CHICKENS
HAVE EGGS TO LAY.

SALLY CLUCKS,
QUEENIE SINGS,
GERTRUDE SQUAWKS
AND FLAPS HER WINGS.

AN EGG A DAY
IS LAID WITH CARE
IN NESTS OF STRAW
AND HORSE'S HAIR.

THE EGGS ARE BROWN
AND WARM TO TOUCH,
ABIGAIL SAYS
THANKS SO MUCH.

SALLY CLUCKS,
QUEENIE SINGS,
GERTRUDE SQUAWKS
AND FLAPS HER WINGS.

AND OFF THEY SEARCH
THE YARD FOR BUGS,
TO SCRATCH FOR WORMS,
GRUBS AND SLUGS.

THEY CHANCE TO PLAY
AND EXERCISE,
TO CHASE A MOTH
OR LIZARD PRIZE.

THEY PECK AND PECK,
THEY PREEN AND PREEN,
THEY LIKE TO LAZE
IN PASTURE GREEN.

SALLY CLUCKS,
QUEENIE SINGS,
GERTRUDE SQUAWKS
AND FLAPS HER WINGS.

THE
END

MORE QUICKTURTLE BOOKS BY MARY AND RICHARD RENSBERRY

GOBLIN'S GOOP
CHRISTMAS CHRISTMAS EVERYDAY
HOW THE SNAKE GOT IT'S TAIL
I WISH IT WERE CHRISTMAS
IF I WERE A CATERPILLAR
IF I WERE A GARDEN
MONSTER MONSTER
COLORS TALK
WAKE'S DAY

AVAILABLE AT AMAZON BOOKS

Made in the USA
Columbia, SC
10 May 2018